CW00801638

BOULAR'S
Great Adventure to Canada

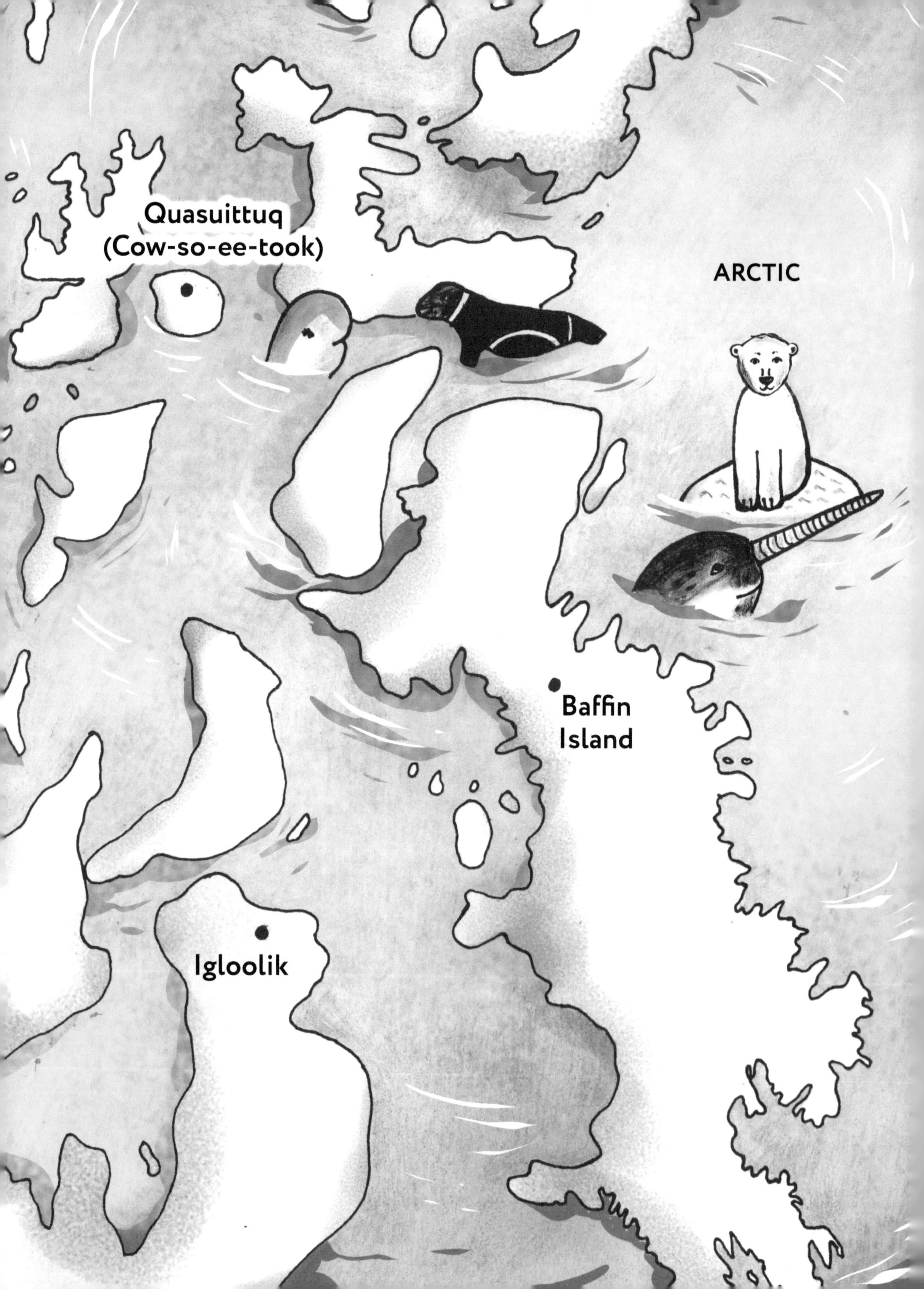
Quasuittuq
(Cow-so-ee-took)
ARCTIC
Baffin
Island
Igloolik

Igloolik
Prince
Charles
Island
Baffin
Island
Whale
Cove
HUDSON BAY
Churchill

BOULAR'S
Great Adventure to Canada

PJ FLETCHER

ISBN: 978-1-80227-662-6 (hbk)
ISBN: 978-1-80227-149-2 (pbk)
ISBN: 978-1-80227-150-8 (ebk)

Dedication

This book is dedicated to my wonderful mum Pauline Winder (1st August 1952 – 22nd December 2019).

My mum was my inspiration and the sole reason I finished my book after starting it ten years ago.

I could not have wished for a better mum; your love and kindness will always shine, and you will never be forgotten.

Acknowledgements

I would also like to thank my family and friends who have supported, encouraged, and believed in me. Thank you for all you love and kindness.

Not forgetting my wonderful dog Fletcher, I could not have wished for a better dog, and also all my other rescue pet family.

Life is about surrounding yourself with love and following your dreams no matter how long it takes – it is the journey that matters.

Contents

Introduction

THIS IS THE STORY of a polar bear called Boular, who lives in the Arctic with his mum, brother and grandfather – The Lord of the Arctic.

Boular really wants to go on an adventure and travel the world, as he has heard so many stories of his grandfather's travels.

Together with his best friend Montgomery the narwhal, they embark on a great adventure to Canada to visit relatives. But most importantly, to try and get help to save their home, which is disappearing due to climate change.

The story is about hope and adventure, making new friends along the way, learning about different places and animals.

There are between 20,000–25,000 polar bears left around the Arctic, and scientists say if we do not act quickly to tackle climate change, polar bears will be wiped out by the end of the century. It is critical that we do our best to help Boular on his quest to save the Arctic.

I hope that you enjoy reading *Boular's Great Adventure to Canada* and that he has many more adventures travelling to other countries with you.

Part of the proceeds from this book will go to help polar bears and the fight against climate change. By purchasing this book, you will be supporting this cause as a contribution for every book sold will be made to Greener Every Day, a charity that plants trees to help combat climate change.

1 x 8 = 8
2 x 8 = 16
3 x 8 = 24
4 x 8 = 32
5 x 8 = 40
6 x 8 = 48
7 x 8 = 56
8 x 8 = 64
9 x 8 = 72
10 x 8 = 80

CHAPTER ONE

Meet Boular

"BOULAR, PAY ATTENTION!" said Mr Kookoo in a stern voice.

Boular was sat in another boring maths lesson, wishing he were on some great adventure with his friend Montgomery the whale, not just an ordinary whale but a narwhal. Mr Kookoo, the arctic fox, was teaching multiplications which Boular hated. Whilst Mr Kookoo was teaching the class the 8 times table, Boular was thinking about how he could go on his great adventure and see some of the world. His grandfather, who was known as Lord of the Arctic, had told him about faraway lands that had different creatures and food and spoke in strange languages, which Boular so longed to see and experience. Boular loved geography classes and learning about different countries, and hoped that, when he grew up, he might see some of the amazing places that he had been taught, and his grandfather had spoken about.

Boular's home was very cold and mainly made of ice and snow that was gradually melting away. His mother said that they might have to find somewhere else to live one day, and it was something to do with humans causing it. She said they might have to move near their family in Alaska, Canada, Greenland or Norway.

Boular was the eldest of two cubs; his brother Nanou was ten months old. They enjoyed playing hide and seek in the snow. Nanou was his mother's favourite. Well, that is what Boular thought, as he was always good and enjoyed school, while Boular was always getting told off for not doing his homework, and his mother thought Boular could try harder. Boular just wanted to go on his great adventure around the world, while his mother thought he should stop dreaming and concentrate more on his schoolwork. But Boular had his heart set on seeing the world, and most importantly, saving his home before it disappeared!

MAP

CHAPTER TWO

Sad Goodbyes

ONE DAY BOULAR DECIDED the time had come to go and see the distant lands that his grandfather had told him about.

"Montgomery, do you know that I am old enough now to go on our adventure? Why don't we go to Canada to visit my relatives and get help before our home disappears?"

Montgomery thought it was a splendid idea and decided to go and speak to Walter the walrus, who was incredibly old and wise, and told them what to take and prepare for their journey. Boular was extremely excited and asked his mother and grandfather if he could go and get help from his family in Canada. His grandfather, The Lord of the Arctic, was so happy to hear of Boular's news and immensely proud of his courageous grandson, who he fondly referred to as his little white bear.

The date was set, and Boular's family decided to have a big party to celebrate his new adventure. Boular's and Montgomery's friends were there to wish them luck, cakes were eaten, and games were played. Boular could not believe that it was really going to happen. He had heard so much about Canada from his grandfather that he felt he already knew the place. He knew that it was cold, but nothing that he was not used to, living in the Arctic!

Good Luck

CHAPTER THREE

Off to Canada

THE MOMENTOUS DAY had come for Boular to leave his home and embark on his adventure with Montgomery. All their family and friends were there to say goodbye and to wish them luck on their travels. Boular's mother was extremely sad to see Boular leave home, but equally proud and happy for Boular to go on his adventure to discover the world and try to get help to save their home.

"Be careful, Boular, and don't forget to tell Aunt Hatty to let me know you have arrived safely and to feed you well."

Not long after a tearful farewell with flags flying, Boular and Montgomery set off in the icy waters of the Arctic. They were swimming along when they were rudely interrupted by a cheeky seal.

"Alright, gents, where might you be going?" asked the seal.

Boular, who was amused by the cheeky seal, replied, "Why might it be of interest to you?"

"Well," said the seal, "I might be able to assist you with a short-cut."

Boular and Montgomery looked at one another and nodded.

"So..." said Boular.

"Ziggy is my name," replied the seal.

"So, Ziggy, are you offering to show us the way to Canada?" asked Boular.

"Absolutely. At your service," Ziggy replied, smiling.

"Sorry for my friend's bad manners," interrupted Montgomery. "I am Montgomery, and this is Boular".

"Nice to meet you," replied Ziggy. "Well, gents, shall we begin as we have a long way to go? Have you got plenty of food?" asked Ziggy.

"Of course," answered Boular. "My mother has made enough cakes and fish sandwiches to last us for days."

Spotted Seal
Hooded Seal
Bearded Seal
Ringed Seal
Harp Seal
Ribbon Seal

"Well, I don't mind if I do – I'm starving!" replied Ziggy with a cheeky smile.

They found a floating iceberg to rest and eat while they looked at a map for directions.

"So, what kind of seal are you?" Boular asked inquisitively.

"Why don't you know?" replied Ziggy.

"Well," said Boular, slightly embarrassed. "I know there are a few kinds that live in the Arctic, but I get confused."

"I am a ribbon seal, and I'm the fastest seal in the Arctic, might I add! I always win the seal race every year," Ziggy replied, with a big smile on his face. "Did you know there are six types of seals in the Arctic?"

"That many?" replied Boular, surprised. "No wonder I get confused!!"

"Yes, there's harp, hooded, ringed, bearded, spotted and ribbon – like me."

"Well, that's a whole lot of seals," said Montgomery.

"I know," replied Ziggy, "and we need to eat a whole lot of fish!"

CHAPTER FOUR

Cow-so-ee-took

FINALLY, AFTER A LOT of food and rest, Boular, Montgomery, and Ziggy started their epic journey from the Arctic to Canada. The journey would take them many days and would be dangerous along the way. They would have to watch out for orca whales, because they are not very friendly. They were heading for a place in Canada called Churchill, on Hudson Bay, where Boular's Aunt Hatty, his mum's sister, lived with her husband Joe and his two cousins. He had heard so many stories about his family in Canada but had never been fortunate to meet them. Boular's mother told him that Canada was an extremely popular place for polar bears to live. Boular was incredibly excited to meet his family and to visit another country he had never been to before.

"Canada is a big place," said Ziggy.

"How do you know?" Boular asked. "Have you ever been?"

"Well, only the once," replied Ziggy. "I went with my father a few years ago. All I can remember is that it took a long time, and I was very tired!!"

"Well," said Montgomery, "does anyone know the capital of Canada?"

"No," Ziggy replied.

"Is it Toronto?" asked Boular.

"No, but good guess," replied Montgomery. "It's Ottawa."

"I have never heard of that place," said Boular.

"No worries," answered Montgomery. "It's good to learn something new each day, and it's part of the adventure. Talking about adventures, we have a big journey in front of us and need to get as far as we can before nightfall."

They set off from the Arctic Ocean, which was big and cold and had been their home. They were heading to a place called Qausuittuq, pronounced Cow-soo-ee-took, which means 'a place where the sun does not rise' on the island of Bathurst, north of Canada.

"By the time we get there, we will need a rest," Ziggy said, laughing.

They had been swimming for quite a while when they heard singing. They looked behind them, and it was a beluga whale.

"Sorry, I didn't mean to startle you," said the beluga whale.

"No, you didn't," Boular replied. "In fact, it's nice to hear singing; it reminds me of my mother."

"Why, thank you. Sorry, where are my manners? My name is Betty, and I know what you are thinking, Betty the beluga whale, haha, very funny. I know – it's my father's fault; it was his favourite grandmother's name," said Betty.

"Well, I think it's a very nice name and suits you," Boular replied with a smile.

"Where are you going?" asked Betty.

"To Canada," replied Ziggy.

"Oh, that's a long way," Betty said, surprised.

"We are going on an adventure," Boular replied with a proud look on his face.

"Wow, really?" said Betty.

"Well, we're also going to see my family in Canada at

Hudson Bay, as we need their help to save our home," Boular answered with a hopeful smile.

"I think that sounds amazing!" replied Betty.

"Would you like to join us?" Boular asked.

"I would love to," answered Betty excitedly.

So, the four of them smiled at one another and started swimming again.

After what seemed like forever, they saw in the distance the island of Bathurst.

"There it is, Cow-soo-ee-took," said Montgomery.

"At last," replied Ziggy. "I'm starving!!"

As they arrived at the shore, they were greeted by a caribou.

"Welcome to Cow-soo-ee-took."

"Why, thank you," Boular said with a big smile.

"Have you been travelling for a while?" asked the caribou.

"Well, it's a long story," replied Boular. "We'll tell you over dinner."

"I'm starving," said Ziggy – again.

"How about if I make you one of our local, speciality stews?" offered the caribou.

"That's very kind you," answered Betty happily.

"Sorry, excuse my manners, my name is Vincent, and I'm a Peary caribou."

"Pleased to meet you," Boular, Montgomery, Ziggy and Betty replied in unison.

Whilst Vincent was cooking dinner, he started telling them about the island and that it was part of Canada and a National Park.

"What's a National Park?" Betty asked inquisitively.

"An area that's natural – you know, with trees and the animals that live there are protected," replied Vincent.

"Protected!" said Ziggy, alarmed. "From whom?"

"Why humans, of course!" answered Vincent.

"Humans over time have liked to hunt animals and fish, even whales like me!" said Montgomery.

"Yes, unfortunately," Vincent replied sadly.

"But it's not just animals," said Montgomery. "Trees too! Humans have cut down many trees so that animals don't have homes."

"That's so sad," Boular replied. "Is that why the ice is melting away in the Arctic like my mother told me?"

"Yes, exactly, as trees help the planet with oxygen," answered Vincent.

"Humans are destroying the planet, so that's why we might have to move?" Boular asked.

"Yes," replied Vincent.

"Why are they doing it?" asked Boular.

"Who knows, maybe they just don't care," said Vincent.

They all sat there quietly, looking at one another sadly.

"Well, it's lucky that you live here, Vincent," Boular said with a smile.

"I know," Vincent replied.

He had almost finished cooking when some of his friends turned up, wondering who Vincent's new friends were.

"These are my friends from the Arctic, travelling to Hudson Bay," said Vincent. "This is Boular, Montgomery, Ziggy and Betty," he continued, introducing them all.

"Hello, nice to meet you," replied the muskox. "My name is Milo, and these are my friends," he said, pointing to the arctic fox, the snowy owl and another muskox.

"Pleased to meet you all," Boular said with a big smile.

They all sat down and ate Vincent's delicious stew and told stories of their homelands until everyone got tired and needed to get some sleep.

"Goodnight everyone," said Boular.

map

CHAPTER FIVE

Escaping Danger

THE NEXT DAY THEY woke up bright and early, ready to start another day of their adventure. They waved everyone goodbye and thanked Vincent for kindly looking after them.

"They were a nice bunch," said Ziggy.

"Yes, and what a beautiful place they live in," Betty replied cheerfully.

"How nice to live somewhere and know that you're safe," Boular said with a smile.

"Very true," Montgomery replied as they continued their journey through the icy waters.

"We're heading south," directed Ziggy.

After what seemed like a long tiresome swim, they decided to have a rest and eat some cake that Boular's mother had made.

"Why this is the best cake I have ever eaten!" Betty said with a big smile.

"Thank you," replied Boular. "My mother does make amazing cakes. I will miss her so much, but she knows how much I wanted to go and see new places."

"Why did you want to travel?" asked Betty.

"Well, my grandfather, the Lord of the Arctic, told me stories of his travels to faraway lands, and I just thought how amazing it would be to see different places. Plus, we might have to find somewhere else to live as our home is disappearing," answered Boular.

"Really? That's so sad. I've never really travelled before either," said Betty.

"Well, it's a good thing that we met you," replied Boular. "We can explore the world together!"

As they looked at the map deciding which way to go, Ziggy noticed something in the distance.

"What is that?" asked Ziggy.

"I'm not exactly sure, but I think I saw something black and white in the distance over there, near the island," Boular replied, looking concerned.

"What do you think it could be?" asked Ziggy, who looked worried.

Montgomery had a look and said, "Orcas!"

"You mean orca whales?" Betty asked in a nervous voice.

"Yes," answered Montgomery.

"Aren't they the one's that my grandfather told me to avoid?" asked Boular.

"Yes," replied Montgomery, who was a whale of a few words.

"I don't like orcas," said Ziggy, "or killer whales, as my father calls them."

"We need to avoid them," Montgomery replied in a concerned voice.

"Well, what if we stay here eating cake and pretend that we haven't seen them?" suggested Betty.

"They're coming closer," said Ziggy, looking rather alarmed.

"Right, this is what we're going to do," suggested Boular, who was feeling slightly courageous. "You lot are going to swim quietly over there and hide behind those rocks," Boular said, pointing to his left, "while I am going to swim over and distract them."

"You can't do that; it's too dangerous!" replied Ziggy, who was frightened.

"Listen," said Boular. "My grandfather is Lord of the Arctic, and I'm not going to let some orca whales hurt my friends. I'm a polar bear!!" Boular said proudly.

Whilst Boular started to swim towards the orca's, Montgomery, Betty and Ziggy quietly hid behind the rocks. Now Boular would be lying if he did not say that he was a little bit scared, but he needed to protect his friends. As he got closer, he could see and hear them fiercely blowing water into the air.

"Why, if it isn't a small polar bear!" said one of the orca whales with a sarcastic laugh to the others. "So, what brings a young polar bear here on his own?"

"Why, I'm not on my own," Boular replied confidentially.

The whales looked at one another, confused.

"No, I'm here with my grandfather," replied Boular.

"Your grandfather?" questioned the orca whale.

"Yes," said Boular. "You might know him. He's known as the Lord of the Arctic," Boular replied with a big smile.

"Why yes," answered the orca. "We've heard of your grandfather. He's a legend: big and fierce," said the orca.

"Yes, that's right," replied Boular, "and he's around here somewhere."

"Well," said the orcas, looking worried. "We were just passing; give our regards to your grandfather."

"Oh, I will," replied Boular with a big smile.

With that, the orcas turned and swam away.

Boular swam back to his friends, who were still hiding behind the rocks.

"So," asked Ziggy, "what happened?"

"Well, let's just say that I don't think they will be bothering us again," replied Boular.

"So, does that mean we can continue the journey?" asked Betty.

"Yes, that's right, Betty," Boular replied.

They all looked at one another, smiled with relief and ate more cake to celebrate.

Canada Lynx
Canadian Moose
Bowhead Whale

CHAPTER SIX

The Inuit

TODAY THEY WERE HEADING towards Baffin Island, and the journey seemed easier with plenty of cake in their bellies. They were casually swimming along, passing schools of fish.

"Now, this is the life," said Ziggy.

"I say," replied Boular, in a happy mood after getting rid of the orca whales.

"Shouldn't take long now to get there. The island of Baffin is home to the Inuit," stated Montgomery.

"What are the Inuit?" asked Betty, looking very confused.

"Why they are indigenous people," answered Montgomery.

"Oh," replied Betty, looking even more confused.

"What Montgomery is trying to say, Betty, is that they come from that particular place – like we come from the Arctic," explained Boular.

"Oh, I see," replied Betty.

"Just a fancy word," Boular said with a kind smile.

"Indid-you-what?" asked Betty.

"Indigenous," Montgomery replied.

"Oh," said Betty. "Explain that to me again."

"The best way to explain it is animals and people that live in certain places," answered Boular. "So, for example, Canada, where we're heading, well their indigenous animals are the Canadian lynx – which is a big cat – moose – a bit like Vincent the caribou, but with big horns – and also beluga whales like you Betty."

"So, you mean there's more like me in Canada?" asked Betty, looking surprised.

"Yes, Betty," replied Boular with a big smile.

"Oh, I just thought that we only lived in the Arctic," replied Betty.

"No," Boular said with a big smile.

"Why, aren't I lucky?" replied Betty, smiling back at Boular.

"Anyway, most importantly, do the Inuit eat us?" asked Ziggy, concerned.

"Will we be safe there?" Boular said, looking worried.

"Well, they do like to eat seals and whales, but hopefully, when we arrive, they will have eaten. Plus, we have Boular to protect us," answered Montgomery with a reassuring smile.

They swam a little bit further before seeing the island in the distance.

"There it is," exclaimed Montgomery. "Baffin Island."

They had been swimming for a while, and Ziggy was getting hungry and looking forward to a rest. When they arrived at the shore, they could see a few whales close by.

"What kind of whales are they?" asked Betty.

"Why, they are bowhead whales," replied Montgomery.

Boular was so proud to be Montgomery's friend and so glad that he came along on the journey, as he was so knowledgeable.

"How do you know and remember all this stuff?" Ziggy asked.

"My father and grandfather taught me," answered Montgomery.

As they got closer, Montgomery decided to go over and have a chat with the bowhead whales to see if he could find out some information about the island. A little while later, he returned.

"Well, what did they say?" asked Ziggy.

"They said the best place to go and rest on the island is around the bay. It's quiet, and the Inuit aren't that close by, so we should be safe there."

They all followed Montgomery around the bay to a lovely shore, which seemed quiet with a few houses in the distance.

After a good rest and something to eat, they decided not to stay and take the risk of being seen by the Inuit.

"Where are we going now?" asked Betty.

"We are heading to a place called Igloolik, Betty," replied Boular. "Just for a quick rest and bite to eat."

"More cake?" asked Betty with a big smile.

"Yes, more cake Betty, and then to Prince Charles Island to stay overnight," Boular replied.

The journey took quite some time, and Betty was getting weary.

"How much further now?" asked Betty.

"Not far," replied Boular.

After what seemed like forever to Betty, they finally arrived at the shores of Igoolik.

"Thank goodness for that!" exclaimed Betty. "Why did I allow you to talk me into this journey?" Betty asked.

Ziggy laughed.

"What?" said Betty.

"We didn't make you come with us," replied Ziggy.

"Sorry Betty, we thought that you wanted to come with us on our adventure," Boular answered, looking upset.

"Oh, I'm sorry, guys," Betty said, feeling bad. "I'm just tired; I will feel better once I have had a good night's sleep."

"No problem," replied Boular, with a gentle smile.

"Well, I think we all have done incredibly well," said Montgomery. "It takes a lot of courage to leave your home and go somewhere new."

"But I'm sure that it will be worth it, Betty," replied Boular with a smile. "As my grandfather told me, it's a big world out there, and it's always good to go on adventures and see and learn new things and have stories to tell friends and family."

"You're right," said Betty and tucked into some cake.

CHAPTER SEVEN

Horace and Friends

AFTER A GOOD REST at Igoolik, Boular and his friends decided to swim to Prince Charles Island before nightfall.

"That was a nice little place," said Betty, who felt better for having a rest and cake.

"Igoolik is a nice small place; luckily, we didn't see any of the Inuit," replied Boular.

"Or fortunately, they never saw us!" Montgomery said, relieved. "Do you know what Igloolik means?" he asked.

"No, I don't know," they all replied.

"There is a house here," answered Montgomery.

"Where? I don't see a house," Betty asked.

"No, that's what Igoolik means – there is a house here," replied Montgomery smiling.

"Oh," Betty laughed, realising what she had said.

"It's a small place where the Inuit live," replied Montgomery.

"A bit like Baffin?" asked Ziggy.

"Yes, kind of, but much smaller," answered Montgomery.

"What, smaller people?" Betty asked.

"No, I mean a smaller island, Betty," Montgomery said with a smile. "Lots of animals live there, such as walrus, seals, beluga whales and polar bears."

"Just like being at home," Boular replied.

At that very moment, Ziggy almost bumped into a walrus.

"Oh, I'm so sorry, I wasn't looking where I was going," Ziggy said, looking surprised.

"That's quite alright," replied the walrus. "Did I hear you say that you had been to Igoolik?" he asked.

"That's right," replied Boular.

"Why, that's where I live. Lovely place, a little small, that's why I like to go and see my friends over at Prince Charles Island or POW as it's known." said the walrus.

"Really? That's where we're heading!" replied Boular.

"Well, I can show you the way if you like," offered the walrus. "Oh, by the way, my name is Horace," he added.

"Nice to meet you, Horace," replied Boular, Betty, Ziggy and Montgomery.

On the way to Prince Charles Island, Boular told Horace about their adventure to Canada to see his Aunt Hatty, about the Arctic and his grandfather, the Lord of The Arctic, who had inspired him to travel. He also talked about the ice melting due to humans and that they might soon have to move and find somewhere else to live.

"Oh dear," said Horace. "That's what I heard from friends too, that the Arctic is disappearing, and you're right; it has something to do with humans," replied Horace looking sad.

"Really, but how?" asked Betty.

"Well, it's a thing called climate change, which is causing all sorts of problems," answered Horace. "The sea's getting warmer, icebergs are melting, the sea's rising, there are extreme weather and temperatures. Why, if we carry on, I'm sure that nobody will have anywhere to live!" said Horace, with a worried look in his eye.

"But why can't they stop and see what they're doing?" asked Boular, concerned.

"Who knows?" replied Horace. "Maybe because it doesn't affect where they live, so they don't know and don't have to think about what they're doing."

"Well, someone needs to tell them! Show them what they're doing and the damage they're causing and that some of us won't have homes," exclaimed Boular.

"You're right," said Montgomery, who could see that Boular was getting upset.

"I'm sure that your Aunt Hatty will be able to help when we get to Churchill," replied Montgomery, trying to reassure his friend.

They were almost at Prince Charles Island and could see a group of walruses and other animals waiting near the shore.

"Oh, look, there are my friends. It's Albert's birthday today, and he's having a party if you would like to join us," asked Horace.

"Why, that's very kind," replied Boular.

"We would love to," said Betty with a big smile, thinking about the possibility of cake.

"Don't worry," replied Horace, "there are no humans on this island, just us, so we can make as much noise as we want."

That evening they ate like kings; there was so much food that Ziggy could not believe his eyes! Albert was happy to see his friend Horace and his new friends. There were a lot of animals at the party: walruses, beavers, deer, otters and a big black bear called Honey. Boular had never seen so many animals together! He thought that his and Montgomery's party was big, but it was nothing compared to this. He could not believe that there were other bears besides polar bears.

"Sorry, Honey, I never realised that there were other types of bears," said Boular.

"Why yes," replied Honey. "There are black bears like myself, but then Canada also has grizzly bears, brown bears, cinnamon bears and Kermode bears."

"That's a whole lot of bears!" Boular said with a smile.

"I know, but at Churchill, where you're going, there are a lot of polar bears just like you, so you will be fine," Honey replied, smiling back.

"Yes, I can't wait to meet my aunt and uncle and cousins," Boular said happily.

Cinnamon Bear
Kermode Bear
Black Bear
Grizzly Bear
Brown Bear

After what seemed like hours of playing games and eating and, of course, lots of cake, Boular decided that he needed some rest before his big day tomorrow. He was so excited about meeting his family.

"Thank you so much, Horace, for letting us join your friend's party; it's been so much fun. But tomorrow is going to be a big day, so we must get some rest," said Boular.

"Absolutely," replied Horace with a smile. "I'm glad that you enjoyed yourselves."

"Goodnight everyone, and happy birthday Albert. Thank you for letting us celebrate your birthday," Boular said to Albert and his friends.

"You're very welcome," replied Albert.

CHAPTER EIGHT

Whale Cove

TODAY WAS BOULAR'S big day. He could not believe he was going to meet his family and had hardly slept with excitement! They all had their breakfast and were about to leave when they heard Horace and Albert's voices, who were coming to say goodbye.

"Enjoy your time with your family," said Horace.

"Don't forget if you're ever passing to come and see us; you're always welcome," Albert said with a smile.

"Thank you," replied Boular, Montgomery, Ziggy and Betty.

They all stood waving goodbye at the shore as Boular and his friends swam off to sea.

"Can't believe that I am finally going to meet my Aunt Hatty," Boular said excitedly.

"I bet," replied Ziggy.

"Yes, we will swim down the north-western passage to Whale Cove and then to Churchill," stated Montgomery. "I think you will particularly like Whale Cove, Betty," he added.

"Why? asked Betty. "Are we going to have cake there?"

"Betty, surely you ate enough cake yesterday at the party to last you a week!" Boular answered, smiling.

"Why a whale can never have enough cake," laughed Betty.

"No, because Whale Cove is named after you, Betty," said Montgomery.

"Me?" asked Betty, feeling special. "Why me? They don't even know me!" she said, surprised.

"No, not you in particular, Betty, but rather, beluga whales," replied Montgomery.

"What, beluga whales? There are going to be beluga whales just like me?" asked Betty excitedly.

"Why yes," Montgomery replied with a big smile.

"I can't believe it, beluga whales just like me! I might make some new friends," said Betty.

"I'm sure you will, Betty," Boular replied.

With that, Betty no longer felt tired, and she was looking forward to going to Whale Cove.

The sea was quite choppy with waves, and after what seemed like hours of swimming, they finally were in Hudson Bay and could see land.

"Is that Whale Cove?" asked Betty, beaming with excitement.

"Yes, that's right," answered Montgomery.

On approaching land, the sea began to settle and suddenly became busy with fish, and even some seals were swimming past.

"Well, I think I'm going to like Hudson Bay," Ziggy said with a cheeky smile.

As they got closer to Whale Cove, they could see a lot of whales. Betty's face lit up.

"Look, Montgomery, just like you said, lots of beluga whales. I cannot believe it! I've never seen so many before." Betty was almost bursting with excitement!

"It's like a big beluga party!" said Ziggy.

"Absolutely," replied Boular, who felt so happy for Betty.

Once arriving at the shore, Betty began chatting to a couple of friendly beluga whales, Noah and Bella, who were brother and sister. Betty was having such a lovely time, chatting to them and telling them about the Arctic and how she met Boular, Montgomery and Ziggy and their adventure of going to Cow-soo-ee-took, Baffin, Igoolik and POW and how they escaped the orcas. Bella and Noah were so intrigued by Betty and her story that they asked her if she would like to join them and meet some of their friends.

"Can I, Boular?" asked Betty.

"Sorry Betty, can you what?" replied Boular.

"Can I go and meet Noah and Bella's friends before we leave for Churchill?" Betty asked.

"Of course," replied Boular, who was so happy that Betty was having such a nice time with her new friends. "We will be leaving in an hour, Betty," Boular added as he could not wait to meet his family.

Betty swam off excitedly with her new friends while Boular, Ziggy and Montgomery rested at the shore.

Betty returned an hour later, ready for the final part of the journey. Noah and Bella came to wave goodbye to Betty.

"Why don't you come and see us on your way back?" asked Noah, who seemed to have a soft spot for Betty.

Bella smiled, looking at her brother, who had a twinkle in his eye.

"That would be lovely," replied Betty, who was smiling and blushing at Noah.

They said their goodbyes, and as they were swimming away from the shore, Betty turned round to see Noah still waving.

"Why they seemed like a friendly bunch," said Boular.

"They were," replied Betty.

"I had such fun, and their friends were so nice, I didn't want to leave," Betty said with a tear in her eye.

"Listen, Betty," said Boular.

"Yes," replied Betty, with a tear rolling down her face.

"Why don't you go and spend time with your new friends? You have spent a long time with us, and it's not often you come across beluga whales, and I can see that it makes you happy," Boular said, smiling at Betty.

"Really?" replied Betty. "But I feel bad just leaving you guys," said Betty, looking at Boular, Montgomery and Ziggy.

"Listen, Betty; we will always be friends. But seeing you with your new friends and how happy it makes you, I think you should stay if you really want to and have fun," replied Boular. Montgomery and Ziggy nodded in agreement.

"Oh, thank you, Boular, you're the best friend anyone could wish for. Have fun with your family, and I will see you soon," said Betty, kissing him on the cheek and then swimming off towards Noah.

"Did I do the right thing?" Boular asked Montgomery and Ziggy.

They both smiled and nodded in agreement.

"We will miss Betty," said Montgomery, "but we all deserve to be happy".

CHAPTER NINE

Churchill, at Last!

AS THEY SWAM OFF on the final stretch to Churchill, Boular started thinking about his mother and grandfather and how he wished that they were with him right now. But equally, he was looking forward to telling them about his adventure.

They could see Churchill in the distance, and Boular could not contain his excitement.

"We're here; I can't believe that we're really here!" shouted Boular excitedly.

As they swam to the shore, they were greeted by lots of polar bears.

"Welcome, you must be Boular. We've heard so much about you and have been waiting for you to arrive."

Boular felt overwhelmed by all the friendly polar bears.

"Excuse me, but do you know where my Aunt Hatty and Uncle Joe are?" asked Boular.

A voice came from behind him. "Boular, it's us," answered Aunt Hatty.

Boular turned around, smiling at his Aunt, who gave him a big hug.

"Why, Boular, I'm so happy to finally meet you!" said Aunt Hatty.

"What a brave chap you are," said Uncle Joe, "coming all this way to see us."

"Oh," replied Boular. "It's been quite an adventure," and turned smiling at Montgomery and Ziggy. "Also, we need your help as the Arctic is disappearing because of climate change, and I wondered if you might be able to save our home?" asked Boular, feeling hopeful.

"Of course, we will do our best to help you save your home, Boular," answered Aunt Hatty, with a reassuring smile.

That evening they had a huge party to celebrate their arrival with lots of cake.

"Betty would have loved this," said Ziggy.

"Yes, she would," replied Montgomery and Boular with a big smile.

"Finally, we have made it! Thank you so much for sharing the adventure," said Boular.

"You're welcome; I wouldn't have missed it for the world," replied Ziggy, smiling. "That's what friends are for."

"Me too," said Montgomery.

ABOUT THE AUTHOR

PJ FLETCHER lives in the beautiful English Lake District that inspired Beatrix Potter. As an animal lover, she has three rescue dogs from the UK, Spain and Romania, three cats, and is a dedicated vegan.

Fletcher grew up reading Alice in Wonderland and The Jungle Book, and inspired by these, *Boular's Great Adventure in Canada* is the first children's book she has written. Her concern about climate change and its impact on the planet led to the idea for a story of a polar bear who wanted to travel and learn about the world. Fletcher felt it would help make children more aware of the issues surrounding these important matters.

After attending a writer's workshop, with guest speakers Neil Blair and Amanda Craig, about ten years ago in London at Waterstones, Fletcher always intended to complete the book, but life got in the way. She was working in sales and then recruitment until she decided to leave and concentrate more on her writing.

HERE'S MORE ABOUT CLIMATE CHANGE

PLEASE FIND BELOW links to websites offering additional learning on climate change, polar bears and maps of Canada and the Arctic.

www.climatekids.nasa.gov – about climate change
www.polarbearsinternational.org – about polar bears and the Arctic
www.arcticwwf.org – about the Arctic and climate change
www.theglobaleducationproject.org – about animals at risk from climate change
www.earthrangers.com – about helping the planet and animals
www.sciencebuzz.com – about climate change
www.greenereveryday.co.uk – about trees and climate change
www.oceanconservancy.org – about beluga whale conservation
www.oceana.org – about narwhals
www.seaworld.org – about beluga whales
www.uk.whales.org – about beluga whales and other whales
www.oceanwide-expeditions.com – about types of seals in the Arctic
www.intrepidtravel.com – about animals that live in the Arctic
www.worldatlas.com – about animals that live in Canada
www.infoplease.com – map of the Arctic
www.mapsofworld.com – map of Canada

CANADA

BERING SEA
NORTH PACIFIC OCEAN
Alaska
Arctic Circle
Canada
ARCTIC OCEAN + NORTH POLE
Russia
HUDSON BAY
BAFFIN BAY
Greenland

Lightning Source UK Ltd.
Milton Keynes UK
UKHW050659100223
416725UK00003B/138